Rachel has got home from school.

She lets herself in.

There is a note on the kitchen table.

Rachel,

Can you go to the corner shop for me?

We need a few things.

I've left you a list and a £5 note.

Back soon.

Love Mum

xxx

PS I'll do a big shop tomorrow

Shopping list
Small loaf
Shampoo
Fruit for your packed lunch
tomorrow
Tea bags   Quickbrew

5

Rachel finds the bread.

Good! There's a small brown loaf.

She puts it in her basket.

The apples look nice.
The bananas look nice too.

She can't decide. Help!
At last she chooses one of each.

Now she's looking for some shampoo.
She meets her friend, Sophie.

"You have got to try this shampoo," says
Sophie.
"I bought some last week and it's
GORGEOUS!"

Just one more thing – the teabags.

But there's a small problem.

She can't see the kind that her mum likes.

She spends ages looking at the ones on the shelf.

In the end she chooses Special Blend.

Now she has got everything.

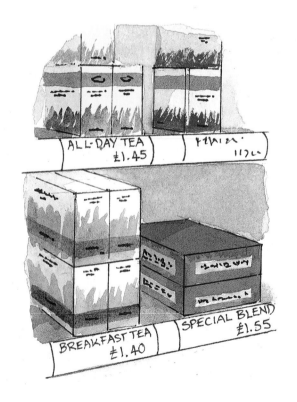

ALL-DAY TEA
£1.45

BREAKFAST TEA
£1.40

SPECIAL BLEND
£1.55

She takes her basket to the checkout.
She is lucky, there is no queue.
The cashier scans her things.

15

"That's £5.10 and your receipt," the cashier says.
But Rachel has got only £5.
What do you think she will do?